This Ladybird Book belongs to:

_____

_____

_____

_____

retold by Audrey Daly
illustrated by Peter Stevenson

Cover illustration by Thea Kliros

Copyright © Ladybird Books USA 1996

Originally published in the United Kingdom by Ladybird Books Ltd © 1993

First American edition by Ladybird Books USA
An Imprint of Penguin USA Inc.
375 Hudson Street, New York, New York 10014

Printed in Great Britain
10 9 8 7 6 5 4 3 2 1

ISBN 0-7214-5645-6

FAVORITE TALES

Tom Thumb

nce upon a time, there lived
a woodsman and his wife.
They were very sad because
they had no children.

"If only we had a child to love,"
said the wife. "I wouldn't mind if
he were as small as my thumb!"

Time passed. At last, they had a son!
This made them both very happy.

Strangely enough, the child was very
small. He never grew any bigger than
a person's thumb! So his parents
named him "Tom Thumb."

One day, Tom's father sighed, "I'm so tired these days. If only Tom were bigger, he could drive the wood cart into the forest for me."

Tom looked at his mother. "I can drive the cart!" he said. "If you will harness the horse, Mother, I'll show you how."

Tom's mother did as he asked. "Now, put me in the horse's ear," said Tom.

A moment later, off went the cart
with Tom tucked in the horse's ear.

When Tom said, "Turn left," the
horse turned left. When Tom said,
"Turn right," the horse turned right.

Two men strolling through the forest saw Tom's cart. Surprised to see this curious sight, they decided to follow.

The cart stopped and Tom's father appeared. The two men watched as Tom's father took his tiny son out of the horse's ear.

The men were amazed. "What a clever little fellow he is," one of them said. "Will you sell him to us?"

"I would never sell him," replied the woodsman. "He is my son."

But Tom whispered, "Sell me to them, Father. It will be an adventure! And I'll be back soon."

Reluctantly, the woodsman agreed. He sold Tom for thirty gold pieces.

The two men set off. One of them slipped Tom into his pocket. "We can put Tom on show in the towns," he declared. "He will make us rich!"

Toward evening, Tom called out, "I need to stretch my legs! May I walk around a little?"

The man put him down. Tom ran away as fast as he could and hid. The men looked everywhere, but Tom had disappeared.

Tom looked for a safe place to sleep.
He soon found an empty snail shell
and curled up inside.

Just as he closed his eyes, he heard
voices nearby. "We'll sneak into the
pastor's house and steal his money!"
said one.

"They must be thieves!" thought
Tom. "Take me with you," he cried
in a loud voice. "I can help you!"

The men were puzzled. They heard a
voice, but they didn't see anyone.
They were astonished when they
found the tiny boy.

The thieves listened to Tom's plan. "I can get in through a crack in the window," he said, "then I'll throw the money down to you."

They went to the pastor's house. Tom climbed up the drainpipe and slipped in through a crack in the window. A moment later, he came out and stood on the ledge. He shouted, "Do you want *all* the money that's here?"

"Sssh!" said the frightened thieves. "You'll wake the whole house!"

Tom shouted even louder. "HOW MUCH MONEY SHOULD I THROW DOWN?"

The cook was sleeping in the next room. She awoke with a start. "What's that noise?" she cried.

When the cook got up
to look, Tom ran to
the barn. There,
he settled down
to sleep in
the hay.

By the time the
cook got downstairs, the
thieves were gone. They had run
away without stealing a penny.

The next morning, the cook went to feed the cow. She picked up the very bundle of hay that Tom was sleeping in and tossed it in the cow's stall.

Tom woke up and found himself being tossed around in the cow's mouth. Then he tumbled down into the cow's stomach.

"Hey!" yelled Tom. "Let me out of here!"

"Help!" the cook cried. "The cow is talking!" Frightened, she ran for the pastor.

"Don't be silly," the pastor told her, looking closely at the cow. "Cows don't talk."

Just then, Tom shouted again, "Help me!" Terrified, the pastor and the cook ran off. Meanwhile, Tom crawled out of the cow's stomach and slipped away.

Tom's troubles were far from over. A hungry wolf was passing by and saw Tom sneaking through the farmyard.

"This will make a tasty little snack," thought the wolf, and he swallowed Tom in one gulp.

Clever Tom quickly thought of a plan. "Wolf," he called, "if you're still hungry, I know where there is a lot of food." And he told the wolf how to get to his very own house, which was not far away.

When they arrived, Tom said, "Just crawl through the drain. It leads to the kitchen, where there is plenty to eat."

The drain was quite small, but the wolf squeezed and pushed and managed to get through.

In the kitchen, the wolf ate and ate
and grew fatter and fatter. So when
he tried to crawl back through the
drain, he no longer fit!

Now Tom began to shout and sing
as loud as he could.

The kitchen door burst open. It was the woodsman and his wife, awakened by the noise.

"A wolf!" cried Tom's father, reaching for his axe.

"Wait, Father!" shouted Tom. "It's me! I'm here, inside the wolf's stomach!"

"Tom!" cried his father. "Don't worry, we'll save you!"

With one blow of his axe, Tom's father killed the wolf. Then, very carefully, he cut a little hole in the wolf's stomach.

Out jumped Tom, safe and sound. "I told you I'd be back soon, Father!" he laughed.

Tom's parents were overjoyed to see him. "We will never part with you again," said his father, "not for all the money in the world."

"And I will never leave home again," promised Tom. "I've had enough adventure to last a lifetime!"

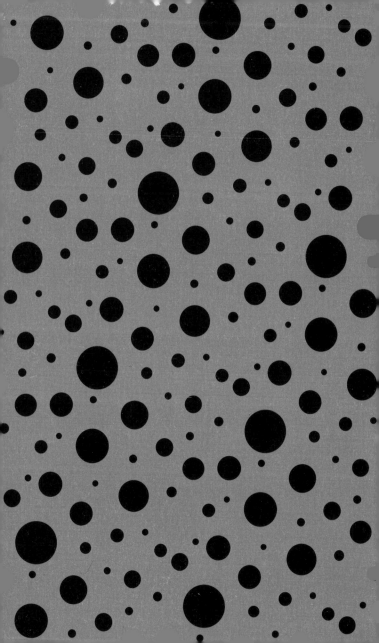